About the Author

A virgin author until he was approaching ninety years of age, Jeremy Raylton has written books for children, two short stories and two historical novels. He used to take walking seriously, completing a thousand miles in several years and also two marathons. As that has become impossible, he fills a comparable part of each day writing, for his own pleasure and, hopefully, the pleasure of those who read his words.

Jeremy Raylton

Berti's Holiday

Bumblebee Books
London

Bumblebee Books is an imprint of
Olympia Publishers.

First Published in 2023

Bumblebee Books
Tallis House
2 Tallis Street
London
EC4Y 0AB

Printed in Great Britain
www.olympiapublishers.com

Dedication

Dan Ranger's illustrations in *Many Mice and a Ginger Cat* begged to be enjoyed in a sequel, and when Berti decided to go on holiday, his adventures were beautifully depicted by Dan.

Acknowledgements

Thanks are due to my sister Rosemary for proofreading yet another of my efforts.

1

Berti and his wife Mary lived in a barn with all the other members of their family. His father and mother were there, along with Berti's children, who now had children of their own. It was a big barn, and there was plenty of room in the holes in the walls for each family to have its own home. Many mice lived in the barn very happily.

The barn was an old one, with stone walls, and there was lots of space between the outer and inner walls, so when one of the mice wanted to leave its family and have a home of its own, there was always a suitable place not far away.

Every summer, the farmer filled the barn with lovely freshly-cut hay, and the mice used this to make their homes draught-proof and really comfortable. During the winter, the hay was gradually taken to feed the farmer's cows and sheep, but there was always enough left for the mice to be able to change the hay in their homes every so often.

Close to the barn was the cottage where a nice man and his sister lived. He had been a storekeeper in the town; he had welcomed Berti and his family to his store when they had to leave the rectory where they used to live. The rector had been happy to give the mice a home, but his wife did not like them and got a cat to chase them away. The mice had been very frightened when the cat came, but it did not chase them at all and even liked to play with the baby mice.

It was more than a year ago when the storekeeper had come to visit his sister Agnes in her cottage, and she had said, "Why do you not leave your store and come and live here with me?"

He had thought that it was a good idea, but he had become very fond of the mice and the cat, and he did not want to leave them if he moved. He was worried that Agnes might not want him to bring them with him.

But Agnes had said that she would like them to come, and that there was plenty of room for the mice in the barn, and that the cat could live in the house. And so Berti and his family, and the cat, had all moved from the store in town to the barn in the country. The mice had been very excited when they were told that they could live in the barn, and the cat had been pleased to find that there was a nice fireplace in the cottage, where it was allowed to lie in front of the fire when it was cold.

The cat was a very beautiful ginger colour. It was very happy in its new home with the storekeeper and Agnes. It was fed very well, and there were some fields and woods only a short distance from the cottage which it could explore when the weather was good. It was very fond of the mice, and often used to play with their babies in the barn. The mice felt very safe with the cat to protect them and sometimes went with it when it went exploring.

One day, Berti and the cat were sitting in the sunshine outside the barn. The cat said to Berti, "The storekeeper and Agnes are going on holiday next week and will be away for ten days."

"What is a holiday?" asked Berti.

"I don't exactly know," said the cat, "but before they leave, they are very excited and when they come back, their skin is browner, and they tell their friends how nice the weather was."

"Where do they go?" asked Berti.

"Usually to the seaside," said the cat.

"What is the seaside?" asked Berti.

"I have no idea," said the cat.

"It might be nice to go on holiday," said Berti. "But I would like to know more about it."

A few days later, the storekeeper put two cases in the car and told the cat that he and Agnes would be away for ten days.

"You must look after the mice while we are away," he said to the cat, "and see that no rats take up residence in our cottage or the barn."

The cat purred its acceptance of these responsibilities and went to tell Berti what the storekeeper had said. Berti said that he and Mary would like to go on holiday on the next day, but the cat said that it might not be safe to go without him to protect them and that he could not leave while the storekeeper was away.

"Alright," said Berti, "but I am going to make plans, and I hope that you will come with us."

The cat purred at the thought of going on holiday.

2

Berti told Mary that the storekeeper and Agnes were going on holiday, and would be away for ten days.

"When are they going?" asked Mary.

"Today," said Berti.

"Where are they going?" asked Mary.

"I don't know," said Berti, "probably to the seaside."

"What is the seaside?" asked Mary.

"I don't know," said Berti.

"You don't know much," said Mary and went inside to prepare the lunch.

Berti had no way of finding out about the seaside, but he was determined to go on holiday. He went and told Mary that they were going on holiday today, to tell the eldest children to look after the young ones, and to pack some food to eat on the journey.

"How long will we be away?" asked Mary.

"I don't know," said Berti and went to tell the cat what he was going to do. The cat said that he would like to go on holiday with them, but that he had told the storekeeper that he would look after the mice and the cottage while he and Agnes were away.

Just before it got dark, Berti and Mary set off on their great adventure. They followed the hedgerows that they knew until they came to some new ones. Berti said that they should continue in the same direction. Because they did not know this area, they travelled much more slowly and in the middle of the night, they stopped by a little stream and ate some of the food that Mary had packed.

"Do you think that we are nearly at the seaside?" she asked.

"I think so," said Berti.

While they were eating their food, two mice came out of the hedgerow and stopped by Berti and Mary. "Where are you going?" they asked.

"To the seaside," said Berti.

The two mice burst out laughing, and Berti asked them what was so funny. They said that they had never been to the seaside but that they had heard that it was very far away and no place for mice to go on holiday.

"Where are you going?" asked Berti.

"To the fair," they replied. "Why don't you come with us?"

"What is a fair?" asked Berti.

"We'll show you, come on," said the fieldmice, and they set off along the hedgerow.

Berti and Mary quickly finished their meal and hurried after their new friends. When they caught up with them, they noticed that they both had empty sacks on their backs. Berti would have liked to ask what they were for, but he thought that it might seem rude to ask.

While they made their way along the hedgerows, the four mice introduced themselves and they all stopped for a moment to shake hands. Berti and Mary found that they were travelling with Tommy and Mopsy.

"That's a funny name," said Tommy, but Mary said that it was a lovely name. She and Mopsy walked on together, telling each other about their homes and families.

Quite soon, when they came to the end of the hedgerow, they saw a very big grass field in front of them. The field was full of big machines and lorries. Although it was still dark, they could see that the machines were painted in bright colours. One or two of the lorries had lights shining through their windows and looked like little houses.

"Is this the fair?" asked Berti. "And if so, why have we come here?"

Tommy told him that during the day lots and lots of people came, the big machines went up and down and round and round, and that there were lots of places where food was sold.

"That is why we come here," said Mopsy. "People drop bits of food everywhere. We pick it up and put it in our sacks. We usually take home enough food for all of the family for almost a week."

"We don't have sacks," said Berti.

"Don't worry," said Tommy. "There are lots of paper bags that people drop."

And so, the four mice made their way very carefully into the fairground. Berti and Mary soon found paper bags and all four mice were soon picking up food. There were several dogs with the lorries that had people in them but they were tied up and the mice could avoid them.

They were so busy collecting food that they did not notice that it was getting light, and Tommy said that it would not be safe to go home in daylight. They found a good hiding place in what seemed to be a little shed and settled down to sleep. They had come a long way and worked hard to fill their sacks and bags, and they were quite tired.

3

The four mice were still fast asleep when a man came into the shed and started opening it up. Luckily, the mice were all together beneath a tarpaulin at the back of the shed, and although they got ready to run for their lives, they were not discovered.

When the man finished, the top half of the front of the shed was open. He and a lady called out, "Come and see the Punch and Judy show." The mice had no idea what that was, but quite a lot of people came and laughed a lot at what the man and lady were doing.

By the middle of the day, the field was full of people. All the big machines that the mice had seen when they arrived in the middle of the night were attracting a lot of customers. The mice could see the fairground, for that is what the field was, through a crack in the shed's wall, and they took it in turns to peep out. One machine consisted of a very tall pole and attached to the top of it were wires with seats on the end. When the pole went round and round, the seats flew round in a big circle and the people sitting in them shouted and screamed with excitement.

Another machine had lots of small cars on a flat floor and the people in them drove the cars round the floor, bumping into the other cars. The biggest machine was very tall. It had little cars holding up to four people and the cars travelled up and down a very narrow track at high speed a long way above the ground. Berti thought that it looked very dangerous, but there was always a long line of people waiting for their turn.

During the day, the mice could not risk leaving the shed but they had plenty of food and Tommy, who had been to the fair several times, said that during the night, they could move to a better place.

By the time that it got dark, all the mice had had several turns looking through the crack and each one had a favourite machine that they wanted to go on, but Tommy said that it was too dangerous and that even if they were not discovered, they could be hurt or killed. Berti thought that he would like to risk it, but he did not tell that to the others.

When all the people had left the fairground, and the machines had been turned off and cleaned, the mice left the Punch and Judy shed and spent some time refilling their sacks and bags with food. The best place to get something was where the stalls which sold food stood, and it was not long before all the mice had filled their containers and also had a good meal.

Berti and Tommy told Mary and Mopsy that they were going to find as good place for tomorrow, and that they should not wander round the fairground while they were away. Some of the dogs might not be tied up, and there might also be cats which were not as friendly as the ginger cat that they knew.

It was not long before Berti and his new friend were successful. At a place where people threw balls and tried to knock coconuts off the tops of sticks, there was a big wall made of bales of straw; Tommy said that this was to stop the balls hitting people who were passing by.

The two mice found a good spot between two of the bales on the top row. From there, they could see almost the whole fairground and lots of machines and tents that they had not seen before. Berti told Tommy to stay there and make a comfortable home a little bit back from the front edge of the bales while he went to fetch Mary and Mopsy.

He thought that he remembered all of the way back, but after a bit he was not sure which way to go. He recognised the caravan, for that is what Tommy had told him the lorries with lights on were called. While he was deciding, the door of the caravan opened and a woman thew out a basinful of water. Luckily, it just missed Berti and he hurried beneath the caravan, where he thought that he would be safe.

From there, he was able to see another caravan that he recognised, and he was soon back at the Punch and Judy shed. He told Mary and Mopsy that he and Tommy had found a very good, safe place, from where they could see all the fairground. They packed away what food they had not eaten and followed Berti.

As they passed one of the caravans, a dog jumped out at them. Luckily, it was attached to the caravan by a chain and could not reach them, but they were very frightened and Mopsy said that she did not want to go any further. Berti said that they could not stay there for when it got light, they would certainly be found, and Mopsy very reluctantly agreed to go on.

They did not lose their way and before it got light, they reached the wall of straw bales and climbed up to the top row. When Mary and Mopsy saw the little house that Tommy had made, they were very surprised, and when he showed them that they could see all the fairground without going outside, they were very happy.

It soon got light and the four mice spent the morning watching the people and the machines. They could not see what happened in the tents, but people often came out of some of them with sandwiches and drinks, and Berti said that it might be easy to find food there when it got dark again. Tommy said that the fair was not always there and that it moved from place to place during the summer; it might pack up and move at any time.

Berti very much wanted to go on one of the machines before the fair moved, but he did not tell the others as he thought that they would say that it was too dangerous. It was very warm and cosy in the straw bales and after they had eaten their lunch, Tommy, Mopsy and Mary fell asleep, and Berti had an opportunity to see if he could get a ride on one of the machines. His favourite one was the little cars that bumped into each other, but he did not think that he could get into one without being seen.

He noticed that the seats on the ends of the wires attached to the pole that went round stayed on the ground before the pole started to go round. He managed to scuttle into one of them without being seen. A man and his young daughter got onto the seat, and before very long, the big pole started to go round and the seat left the ground. Faster and faster, the seat went round the pole, quite high above the ground, and Berti wondered whether he had been wise to get in the seat. But after a bit, he found that he could see out through a hole in the canvas that was round the seat, and he had a wonderful view of the fairground and everything in it. He thought that he would have a lot to tell the others when he got back to the straw bales.

4

The other three mice were still asleep when Berti got back to their nest, but Mary woke up as he came in.

"Where have you been?" she asked him.

"I have been on a ride on that machine with the seats that fly round and round," he said.

"Don't tell me stories," said Mary. "What have you been up to?"

It took Berti some time to convince Mary that he was telling the truth and while he did so, Tommy and Mopsy woke up and heard what he was saying. Mopsy said that she would like to go on the same machine as Berti, but Tommy said that it was too dangerous, supposing the wire broke and the seat fell to the ground.

Mary said that if Berti could do it, she was sure that she could too, but that she would like something that stayed on the ground. Berti said that the little cars that bumped into each other would be alright, but it might be hard to get in one without being seen.

Tommy said that they should all stick together, and that what they should do was wait until that night and then get into one of the cars before it got light next morning. Berti said that it was a good idea and that there would be less chance of being discovered, if they got into two cars. Tommy agreed, and they ate their supper with excitement for tomorrow's adventure.

As soon as it was dark, they left their nest and climbed down the wall of straw bales. Berti led the way to the machine with the little cars. On their way, they passed a tent with a sign at the entrance saying 'Ghost Train'.

"I wonder what that is," said Mary, but Berti said that they could not stop and find out.

There was a man cleaning the little cars when they got there. They waited until he had finished with one that was close to the edge of the track.

"Go now," Berti said to Tommy, and he Tommy and Mopsy scampered across the track and jumped into the little car. Tommy waved at Berti to signal that they were alright there. A short time later, the man had finished cleaning another car, and Berti and Mary got into it without being seen.

"We have a long time to wait here until the rides start again in the morning," said Berti. "We must go to sleep, but I feel quite hungry."

"Then it is a very good thing that I brought a bag of food with me," said Mary. She gave some bread and a bit of cheese to Berti.

The man finished cleaning the cars and switched off the lights, so it was too dark for the mice in one car to see the others in the other car. Berti hoped that Mopsy had taken some food with her, but he and Mary had eaten all of theirs so there was nothing left to take to them, even if he could find them in the dark.

All the mice slept quite comfortably on the floor of their cars, and they only woke up when people started getting into them. They had to avoid the feet, and there seemed to be no way that they could see out, until Berti found that there was a small hole all round the light at the front of the car. He and Mary settled down by the hole, and they hoped that Tommy and Mopsy also had a hole that they could look through.

It was not long before the cars started moving. They moved faster and faster, and Berti and Mary could see all the other cars around theirs. They did not know which one Tommy and Mopsy were in, for all the cars were the same, but Berti saw that they all had the same hole round their lights, so he hoped that their friends would get to see what happened.

Very soon, the cars started hitting each other. Many of the drivers were children, and they enjoyed bumping into the other cars, some of which had their friends in them. Because Berti and Mary were in the very front of their car, they could see when there was going to be a collision. To start with, they were rather frightened and thought that they might get hurt but when they found that the cars were protected by big strong bumpers, they began to enjoy it.

There was very loud music playing, and it was not easy for the mice to hear each other, but Berti managed to tell Mary to look out for Tommy and Mopsy. But although they could see out of their car, they could not see into the other cars through the little holes round the light, so Berti was very surprised when their car hit another one head on and Mary shouted, "There they are!"

"How do you know?" asked Berti.

"Because they have stuck one of their sacks through part of the hole round the light, so that we would know which car they are in."

"What a good idea," said Berti. "If we do the same, they will know that we are in this car."

So Berti pushed the end of their empty food bag through the hole, and several times the cars with the mice in collided, and the mice shrieked with excitement; but the music was so loud that the people in the cars did not hear.

It seemed that the mice would be in the bumper cars all day, but one of the cars broke down and had to be mended. While this was being done, the mice were able to leave the machine without being seen. It was now the middle of the day, and there were a lot of people about, so the mice had to be very careful. Some of the people had dogs, and that made it even more difficult for the mice.

After several quick dashes from one bit of cover to another, they came again to the entrance to the 'Ghost Train'.

"Let's go in here," said Berti. "It is nice and dark and we will not be seen."

"What is a ghost train?" asked Mary.

"I don't know," said Berti.

"I know," said Tommy. "I have been on it."

"What does it do?" asked Mary.

"Come in and you will see," said Tommy. He and Mopsy went through the doorway.

5

Inside the 'Ghost Train' the four mice found that it was almost completely dark; there had been bright sunshine outside, and it was some time before their eyes adjusted. When they did, they saw that it was a long, narrow tunnel with lots of bends in it. There were rails on the floor of the tunnel and little open carriages – with seats for six or eight people – moved slowly along the rails.

"Don't cross the rails," said Berti to Mary. "You might get run over by the little train."

For some time, the mice sat and watched the carriages go by. They heard a lot of screaming from further down the tunnel, but they had no way of knowing what was frightening the passengers. When the lights came on, the carriages stopped and the people got out. Tommy led the mice into one of the carriages and showed them where they could hide until the lights were turned off.

Their carriage quickly filled up with passengers, the lights were turned off and the carriages started to move. The mice climbed onto the little deck on the front of their carriage, where they were hidden from the passengers, but it was so dark that they were not in any danger of being seen.

As the train moved through the tunnel, there were lots of things that made the passengers scream with fright. There was a lighted skeleton around one corner, in another place a door opened and a witch threatened the passengers with her broom, and there were vampire bats. As the train moved on, cobwebs with giant spiders brushed the passengers' faces. The mice were not frightened by any of this. They realised that the witch and the vampire bats were not real. They were used to finding all sorts of things in the woods and hedgerows when it was dark. They thought that the passengers were silly to be afraid.

When the train stopped, the mice got off and cautiously made their way back towards the straw wall. They were taking a shortcut through the back of another stall when they were very frightened to hear guns going off very close to them. They were prepared to make a dash for the next cover when Tommy explained that no one was shooting at them, but at targets some way above their heads. He said that he had been frightened in the same way when he first came to the fair.

The mice had had an exciting day. When they got back to their nest between the straw bales, they were ready for a meal and a rest. While they ate the last of their food, Tommy said that he thought they should go home that night. Berti agreed and said that before they left the fairground, they should fill their sacks and bags with food. Everyone thought that was a good idea. They agreed to start off as soon as it got properly dark.

They were woken by a lot of noise. When they looked out through the gap between the bales, they saw that the  machines were being packed up, and all the tents and other stalls were being taken down. The fair was getting ready to move on. It might be a bit more difficult to get away unseen, but at least there would still be food to be found on the ground where the restaurant tents had been. It would soon be dark and they got ready to leave.

But before they left, a big wagon drew up beside the wall of bales and two men started loading the bales onto the wagon. Naturally, they started with the top row, and the mice only just had time to climb down to the ground before their little home vanished. They had a quick discussion about what they should do, and Tommy said perhaps they should go without the food, for there were people everywhere dismantling the machines, but Berti said that they must take some food back, and he led them to where one of the food stalls had been.

There was plenty there to fill their sacks and bags, and in no time, the mice were on their way home. When they came to where they had met Tommy and Mopsy, Mary asked them whether they would like to spend the night in their barn, but Mopsy said that they needed to get back to their children. So the two couples parted, saying that they would meet up again before long.

Berti and Mary continued on their journey and were almost home when they came upon a small field mouse, all by itself, crying its eyes out.

"What is the matter?" asked Mary.

"I can't find my mummy and daddy," said the little mouse. "They went to the fair and I wanted to meet them when they came back, but I haven't seen them."

"What is your name?" asked Mary.

"I am called Nicky," said the mouse.

"Is your mummy called Mopsy?" asked Mary.

"Yes," said the mouse.

"Well, they have just got back, so you must have missed them. Do you know where your house is?" asked Berti.

"Oh, yes," said the mouse.

"Then if you lead us to your house, I think that they will be there," said Mary.

So Berti and Mary followed Nicky, and before very long, they came to his house. Tommy was just coming out, and he said that he had been going to find Nicky. Tommy and Mopsy thanked Berti and Mary for bringing Nicky home and invited them in for a meal. But Berti said that they should get back to the barn before it got light, but now that they knew where Tommy and his family lived, they would call on them someday soon.

Berti and Mary reached the barn just as it was getting light. The ginger cat was inside, playing with the little mice.

"Did you have a nice holiday?" the cat asked them.

"We had a lovely time," said Berti, "but it wasn't really a holiday."

"Did you go to the sea?" asked the cat.

"No," said Berti.

"We went to a fair," said Mary, "and on the way there, we met a couple of mice who had been to the fair before. They showed us where to find food."

Berti thanked the cat for looking after their children, and offered him some of the food in his bag, but the cat said that he didn't really like bread and apples, so Berti and Mary went to tell their children all about the fair. The ginger cat purred and went to sleep.

6

A few days later, the storekeeper and Agnes returned to the cottage. They were both very brown and were in a very good mood. Agnes stroked the cat and gave it a saucer of milk. Then she went into the barn to see that the mice were alright. Berti was playing with the little ones, and Mary was telling the older children all about their time at the fair. She said that they had met another couple of field mice who had told them that they were going to the fair and had invited Berti and Mary to join them.

"What is a fair?" asked one of the children.

"It is a place where a lot of people come to enjoy themselves on lots of big machines and small stalls," said Mary. "There is lots of food to be found, and we lived in a very comfy little nest between two straw bales."

"Did you go on any of the big machines?" asked another child.

"Yes, two of them," said Mary. "One in little cars that bumped into each other and another on a little railway through a long, dark tunnel."

"Can we go to the fair?" asked the children.

"Perhaps when you are older," said Mary. "Now eat your lunches."

That night, the cat told Berti what he had heard Agnes telling one of their friends. They had been to the seaside and stayed in a house very close to the edge of the sea, which is called the beach and is made of sand. Some days, they sat in things called deckchairs on the beach in the sun, and on others, they went for drives in the car to see big houses, gardens or shops.

Berti said that he would like to go on holiday like that, but the cat said that he could not lie on the beach, where a dog might find him or the sea might drown him. If he went to a big house, there were certain to be mice there who might not want him to come in. And unless the shops that they visited were food shops, which seemed unlikely, what would he do in them?

Berti said that he still wanted to go on holiday, but possibly not to the seaside.

The rest of the summer passed very happily and all too quickly for the mice, and it was soon time to start gathering food to store for the winter months. One day, Berti and Mary and their young children were going along a hedgerow when they bumped into Tommy and Mopsy; they had their children with them, and in no time they were making new friends. Tommy led them to a place where there were a lot of delicious berries, and everyone had lots to eat.

Mary asked Mopsy whether their family would like to spend the winter in the barn, where it was never cold and there were any number of places in the walls to make a home. Mopsy said it was kind of Mary to invite them, but they had a lovely home close by in an old rubber boot; it had a hole in the side, which was why it had been thrown away, but in the foot there was lots of room for the six of them. They were always dry, and cats and foxes could not get to them and eat them. Berti said that they lived with a cat, and that it did not want to eat them. Tommy could not believe that and said that they should watch out in case it changed its mind.

Nicky had made a best friend of one of Berti's children, and he asked whether he could go to the barn with him and spend a few days there. Mary said that if Tommy and Mopsy agreed, it would be fine with them. Mopsy said that she was sure he would be in good hands and hoped that he would be no trouble. All the mice collected berries and soon filled the bags that they had brought with them. Then the two families parted, and Nicky went with Berti's family back to the barn.

To start with, Nicky would go nowhere near the cat, but quite soon, he saw that the other mice were not frightened of it and even let it play with their youngest children. When he went close to the cat for the first time, the cat purred and rolled onto its back, so that Nicky could see that it was not going to hurt him. They soon became good friends, and the cat would swish its tail and let Nicky try to catch it.

Berti and Mary had settled back into the life that they led before their visit to the fair. Some nights, when the smallest mice were put to bed, either Berti or Mary would tell them stories about the fair; they made it seem as though the rides that they had gone on were very dangerous, and their children said how brave they were. They particularly liked the stories about the bumper cars and asked whether the storekeeper's car could go on that machine. Berti said that it was too big and the cars on the machine were special ones.

Berti was very happy with his life in the barn. Mary and his children were with him, they had plenty of food, and in the winter they were never cold. The storekeeper and his wife liked the mice, and the ginger cat made sure that no foxes or rats came near the barn. But although Berti had everything that he wanted from his life, he still wanted to go on a proper holiday.

He told this to Mary, but she said that the trip to the fair was enough for her and that she could not leave the children again so soon. So Berti set about seeing how he could go on a proper holiday.

7

The cottage in which the storekeeper and Agnes lived was down a little lane which led to a small village, and at the other end, the lane joined a big, busy road. Berti sometimes used to sit in the hedge beside the road and watch the traffic that went by. There were always lots of cars and lorries and, every now and then, a bus would come along and stop just a little way from the end of the lane.

People from the village would get on the bus with empty baskets and when the bus came back from the opposite direction, they would get off with full baskets. Sometimes, usually during the summer, families would get on the bus with suitcases instead of shopping baskets, and the children were often carrying buckets and spades. Berti thought that they must be going to the seaside, because they came back browner than when they left.

Berti thought that he could get to the seaside if he got on the bus, and he told the cat his plan. The cat said that the bus might go to other places, and Berti might have to get on another bus to get to the seaside, but Berti said that he would only get on a bus if there were children

with buckets and spades, then he could be certain that the bus was going to the seaside.

When Berti told Mary of his plan she was very angry.

"You will never come back," she said. "You will be eaten by a dog or drowned in the sea, and I shall have to look after all your children by myself. Why do you have to go off looking for the seaside? It is not something that normal mice do."

"Perhaps I am not a normal mouse," replied Berti. "And if I do not come back, you can find a normal mouse and marry him."

Mary burst into tears and went to tell the children that their father was going away to the seaside and would never come back.

"Can I go with him?" one of the elder boys asked. "I could make certain that he came back."

Mary kissed him and said that he was a fine boy, but that she would need his help with the little ones while his father was away.

For several days, Berti went and watched the bus come and go, and he saw that when people with suitcases got on the bus, their cases were put in a place underneath the part where there were seats. He thought that if he could get in there, he would know when they got to the seaside, because the people would come and get their cases out of the locker. He told this plan to the cat, and it said that it was a good plan but that the people might get off the bus a long way from the seaside. Berti said that he could not plan everything.

One sunny day, Berti said goodbye to Mary and the children and said that he would be away for a few days. Mary begged him not to go, but he said that it was something that he had to do, and that he might find that it would be possible for all of them to have a holiday by the sea one day.

8

The cat went with Berti to the place in the hedgerow nearest to where the buses stopped. On his back Berti had a small bag, and in the bag there was a change of clothing and just enough food for a day. He had not wanted to take the clothes as he could have got more food in the bag without them, but Mary had said that if he was going to be killed, she wanted him to look properly dressed when he was dead, otherwise it would reflect badly on the family.

While Berti and the cat waited for the bus to come, a man and woman and two children came and stood by where the bus stopped. The parents had suitcases, and the children had buckets and spades.

"They are going on holiday to the seaside," said Berti. "I will go with them."

The cat and Berti did not have to wait long before the bus came, and when the driver saw that there were suitcases, he got out of the bus and opened the locker. When it was open, the cat ran up to him and rubbed itself against his legs. The driver bent down to stroke the cat, and while his attention was distracted, Berti scampered across the grass and jumped into the locker.

By the time that the driver stopped stroking the cat and loaded the family's cases, Berti was hidden behind some cases that were already in the locker. The driver shut the door, got back into the bus, and it moved away from the stop, gathering speed as it went. It was dark in the locker, and Berti did not dare to explore it in case there was a hole in the floor and he fell out onto the road.

When the bus was out of sight, the cat went back to the barn. Mary had hoped that Berti would come back with it, but the cat told her that he was safely on the bus and that she should not worry.

"Berti is a very sensible mouse," he said, "and I am sure that he will be back safe and sound before very long."

"I hope that you are right," said Mary. "He is a good husband and father; I just wish that he was not so keen to go on holiday to the seaside."

In the locker on the bus, Berti made himself comfortable on some rags that he found; even though it was dark, he could see enough to move about – for, like all mice, he had very good night vision. There was quite a lot of noise from the wheels on the road, and Berti could hear the engine, although it was at the front of the bus and quite a way from the locker.

The bus stopped several times, and some more people got on and some got off, but no one came to get cases from the locker, so Berti knew that the family was still on board. Then, at the next stop, the driver came and unloaded two cases. Berti was not sure whether they belonged to 'his' family, but he could not get out without being seen, so he decided to stay on board and hope that he had done the right thing.

Berti was just about to eat some of his food when the bus stopped again, and he could hear all the passengers getting off. The driver came and opened the locker and took out the only two cases that remained. He then locked the door to the bus and went across the road to a small café, leaving the locker door open. Berti crept cautiously to the edge of the locker and peered out. There was a pile of deckchairs near to the bus, and he ran and hid beneath them.

The bus was parked just off a wide road; on one side, there was a row of houses, and on the other side was what Berti imagined must be the sea. He knew that the sea was water, but he never dreamt that there was so much of it; it was blue, and it began on the other side of a wide strip of golden sand, and it stretched into the distance. Berti thought that the sand must be the beach that he had heard of.

He needed to find somewhere safe, for people kept taking deckchairs off the pile, and he might soon have no hiding place left. Across the road, there was a fine house; it was not a new one. Berti knew that old houses, like the rectory in which he had been brought up, had good places in which to hide.

In one of the windows of the house, there were two signs hanging: one said 'Vacancies' and the other said 'No Dogs'. Berti had no idea what vacancies were, but he thought that it would be a good place to stay in, for if they had no dogs, they might like mice, like the storekeeper and Agnes. He waited until there was no traffic coming in either direction and then ran across the road as quickly as he could.

He crawled under the front gate and found himself in a very pretty little garden. There were lots of flowers and shrubs, and he thought that he could stay there if he had to but he wanted to get into 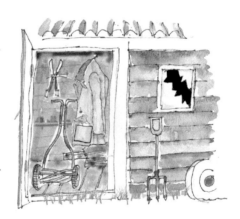 the house. The front door was closed, so he went round the house to the back. There the door was open, and several people were having tea in a much bigger garden than that in front of the house.

There was a big lawn, a small orchard and a shed at the far end. He could not get into the house without being seen, so Berti found somewhere to hide and settled down to wait until they finished their tea. But when they finished the tea and cakes, they started on other drinks, and Berti wondered when he would get into the house.

So, he, very cautiously, made his way down a flower bed to the shed.

The door was shut, but there were lots of holes where the wood had rotted and Berti had no difficulty in getting inside.

There was a window in one side, and Berti looked around to see what was in the shed.

There was a workbench, lots of garden tools, a machine that Berti knew was used to cut the grass and several shelves with boxes of screws and nails in them.

At the back of the shed, there was an old jacket hanging on a peg and looking at Berti out of a hole in one of the pockets, there was another mouse.

"Hello," said Berti.

"Who are you?" said the mouse.

"I am called Berti. What are you called?" said Berti.

"Monty," the mouse replied. "What are you doing here?"

"I am looking for the seaside," said Berti.

"Well, you've found it," said Monty. "It's just across the road."

"Is it a good place for a holiday?" asked Berti.

"Not for us mice," said Monty. "Come up here and I'll tell you all about it."

So Berti climbed up to the jacket and joined Monty in the pocket. Monty said that this shed was a very good place to live, because the people who lived in the house were always having parties in the garden and when they went back into the house, there was always lots of food to be found under the table.

Monty said that he lived alone in the shed and that if Berti wanted to stay with him for a bit, he would be very glad to have the company.

"Would that be a holiday?" asked Berti.

"Definitely," said Monty.

"Good," said Berti.

9

The two mice talked together for a long time. Monty said that he had lived in the shed for two years. Before that, he had lived in the house next door, but they had got a cat and it was not safe to live there any more. Berti said that there was a cat where he lived, but that it liked mice and protected them from foxes and rats. Monty said that it sounded like a very nice cat.

Berti asked Monty whether he was a town mouse. Monty said that he didn't know; he had always lived in the town, so he supposed that he was. Berti said that he and his family had once thought that they were church mice, then they moved into a general store and they became town mice. Then they moved into the country and called themselves country mice, but really they were just field mice who had lived in different places. Monty said that was very confusing, but because he and Berti seemed to be very similar in size, colouring and other respects then perhaps he was a field mouse too. Berti said that he was a very good field mouse.

When the people finished their party in the garden and went into the house, it was almost dark. Monty and Berti left the shed and went across the grass to the table. As Monty had said, there was a lot of food there. They took what they could not eat back to the shed for the next day's meals.

Berti was tired after his exciting day, travelling in the bus and then meeting Monty. He wanted to go to sleep. Monty suggested that he slept in another pocket of the jacket, so that they did not disturb one another. He said, on the next day, he would tell Berti all about the seaside and the other things that people did when they came there on holiday. Berti said how glad he was to have met Monty and thanked him for inviting him to stay in his home. He curled up in his pocket and was asleep before one could say 'cheese'.

Next morning, Monty woke up first and laid out some of their food on one of the shelves. He then went and woke up Berti and told him that breakfast was served. Berti said that he had slept very well and that the jacket pocket was very warm and comfortable. It was raining outside – not hard, but a steady drizzle. Monty said that they would not cut the lawn while it was wet and that they would not be disturbed in the shed.

Until lunch time, Monty told Berti all about the town, and what people did while they were there on holiday. They arranged to go down to the beach that night if it stopped raining, and Monty said that he would take Berti to the fairground and show him all the attractions there. Berti did not tell Monty that he had been to a fair near where he lived, but he looked forward to going to one again. He thought that Monty probably knew more about fairs than he did.

After lunch, they spent the afternoon telling each other about their lives. Monty had lost his mother and father when he was quite young; a dog had discovered where the family was hiding behind a dustbin and the dog's owner had encouraged it to kill the mice. Monty and one of his brothers had escaped, but they had run off in different directions, and they had never seen each other again. Monty had lived in many different places until he found this house. He hoped that he would not have to move again.

Berti told Monty about the countryside where he lived. He said that there were fields with hedgerows round them, and ditches and woods. There were lots of berries and nuts to eat in the summer and store for the winter. The storekeeper's wife fed them when there was no more food in their store. He said that he had a wife, children and grandchildren, and that they all lived in a big barn, where all the families had separate homes in the walls.

He told Monty about the ginger cat and how it not only protected them from foxes but also played with the young mice and let them climb onto its back. He said that he could not imagine a nicer place to live, and it was only because he had heard that holidays were good things that he had left the barn and got on the bus. Monty said that he was very lucky to have such a nice home.

When it got dark, Monty said that he would show Berti the seaside, so that he could tell his family all about it when he went home. They left the shed, crept under the front gate and waited until there were no cars coming. Then they raced across the road and hid under the same pile of deckchairs that had hidden Berti when he got off the bus. It was now a very big pile, because at the end of the day, people had put their chairs back on the pile.

There was no one about. Monty led Berti a little way along the side of the road until they came to the opening of a metal pipe which took rainwater from the road down to the sea. The afternoon drizzle had stopped and there was no water going down the pipe so Monty got in and told Berti to stay close behind him. They went down the sloping pipe for two or three minutes and when they came to the end, they were only a few paces from the sea.

Monty had been down the pipe several times before. He told Berti that they were lucky that the tide was out.

"What is the tide?" asked Berti.

"It is when the sea water comes a long way up the beach. When it does that, it fills the end of the pipe," replied Monty.

"When does it do that?" asked Berti.

"It does it twice every day," said Monty, "but it does it at different times, so you cannot plan a visit to the side of the sea."

Berti looked both ways along the beach and out to sea; he was very proud to have got to the seaside. He could not wait to tell his family all about it. He noticed that the water was coming a bit closer to them all the time. He asked Monty if they should not get back into the pipe before it filled with water, but Monty said that they would go back to the house a different way.

He led Berti along the sand, just above where the sea was coming in. They soon came to what seemed to Berti to be a very long house standing on tall metal feet. It stretched out into the sea, where its feet kept it dry, and Berti could not see the end of it.

"What is this?" he asked Monty.

"It's called a pier," he replied. "In the daytime, and in the evening, lots of people come and play games and eat meals in the rooms."

"Can we get in it?" asked Berti.

"Not from here. We cannot climb these metal feet, but we can get in it at the end by the road."

So the two mice climbed up the sloping beach through the soft sand until they reached the road. There, it was easy to get through the iron gate at the end of the pier and run along it.

10

Berti was very surprised by the number of rooms on the pier. Some were clearly where people ate and they found quite a lot of crumbs there. Other rooms had games in them and at the end of the pier, there were a lot of deckchairs. Berti was getting tired. They had crawled down the pipe, walked along the seaside, up the beach to the road and all the way along the pier. Monty said that they could rest for a bit, but that they must get back to the shed before it got light.

After a short rest, when they ate the crumbs that they had found, they made their way back to the entrance to the pier and along the road. Berti was exhausted. It was a long time since he had walked so far, and he was glad when they crawled under the gate to the big house. He looked up at it and asked Monty what the sign that said 'Vacancies' meant.

"I am not sure," said Monty, "but I have noticed that the sign is sometimes turned round and says 'No Vacancies'."

"Perhaps they sell something called vacancies," said Berti.

"Perhaps," said Monty.

It was almost daylight when the two mice got back to the shed. They were not too tired to have a quick meal, and then they both got into their pockets in the jacket.

"Thank you for showing me the seaside," said Berti.

"Tonight, we'll go to the fair," said Monty.

The two mice slept well. When they woke up, it was just beginning to get dark again. They were both quite hungry, so they ate the rest of the food that they had collected and then they got ready to go out again.

"How do we get to the fair?" asked Berti.

Monty said that it would be quite difficult and dangerous and that he had never actually done it but that he had seen how he thought that it could be done. There were things called trams, sort of buses on rails, which ran along the road to and from the fair, and he thought that it would be possible to climb onto something and get to the fair that way. He knew where the fair was, for at night, you could see the lights and hear the noise, and it was not much further than the pier.

Berti said that if it was that close, he could walk there, but Monty said that there was no cover. They would be seen by people and dogs would get them.

Berti then told Monty that he had been to a fair near his home and that he did not want to risk going to this one. Monty was sad, because he had thought that he could have gone with Berti. But he agreed that it was dangerous and they decided to stay in the shed.

Berti said that he must go home tomorrow or his family would think that he had drowned in the sea. He told Monty how much he had enjoyed his time with him and how grateful he was to him for showing him the real seaside. Monty said that it had been fun to have another mouse to talk to and that any time that Berti wanted to bring his family, they would be welcome to stay with him in the shed.

Berti said nothing for a bit, and then he said, "Why not come with me to my home? You could have your own place in the barn, and there are lots of other mice to meet and things to do."

It did not take Monty long to say how much he would like to go with Berti. He hugged him and said that he was the best thing that had ever happened to him and that he was sure that he would like his wife and family. He did ask whether he could be sure that the cat would not chase him, but Berti said that any friend of his would be a friend of the cat.

So, the two friends ate their supper and planned their next day's journey. Monty was a bit worried about getting on the bus, but Berti said that that was no problem. What did trouble him was not knowing at which stop to get off, as he would not know where any of the passengers with luggage were going. He remembered that the bus had stopped three times on the way to the seaside and he hoped that if they got off on the fourth stop, they would be at the end of the lane where he lived.

In the morning, Berti and Monty ate their breakfast, packed their bags and put some food in their pockets. They made their way cautiously to a place on the opposite side of the road from where Berti had got off the bus and waited under a hedge. Quite soon, a bus arrived, and luckily some of the passengers had luggage to be put in the locker underneath. When it was open and the driver was not looking, they made a rush for the bus and got into the locker without being seen.

There were no rags for them to sit on, and the journey was rather uncomfortable, but they passed the time talking about what Monty could do at the barn. When the bus stopped for the fourth time, they were very relieved that the locker was opened. They shot out of it and across the road into the hedge before they could be caught. The driver did see them, but he had no time to chase mice that were getting off his bus.

Safely across the road and into the hedge, the two mice paused to catch their breath and while they did so, who should turn up but the ginger cat! Monty was terrified, but Berti introduced him and the cat purred his approval of Berti's new friend. The cat told them that he

had come to the hedge each time that he heard a bus approaching, in case he could help them by distracting the driver when they got off. Monty said that it was nice to have such a good friend.

When they got back to the barn, Berti's wife and all their children and grandchildren came to welcome Berti back home, and Berti introduced Monty to all of them. Mary said that it would be nice to have another man in the barn, and two of her unmarried daughters agreed.

Agnes came to the barn and saw that there was a new mouse there; she put a bit of extra food out for the mice.

All the mice wanted to know about Berti's trip to the seaside, and he told them all about it, and how helpful Monty had been.

"Did you actually go in the sea?" asked Mary.

"No, not right in it," said Berti. "It is not something that mice should go in."

"Why not?" asked one of the little ones.

"Because it is very big and very wet, and you would drown," said Berti.

Mary said that she was very proud of him, going so far by himself and that she was glad that he had brought Monty back with him. She said that she would like to go on holiday with Berti sometime soon, but not to the seaside.

The cat nodded its head and purred his agreement.